Gumballs

This Green Light Reader belongs to:

_____

I read it by myself on:

_____

Gumballs

A Mr. and Mrs. Green Adventure

KEITH BAKER

Green Light Readers

HOUGHTON MIFFLIN HARCOURT

Boston   New York

For Betsy and Chris,

Minna and Cooper,

and their sunshine

"Look," said Mrs. Green.
"A gumball-guessing contest!"
"I've never *seen* so many gumballs."
"I've never *imagined* so many,"
 said Mr. Green.

Mr. Green loved
gumballs.
To win them all
would be a dream
come true.

"Let's guess!"
said Mrs. Green.
"This could be
our lucky day."

She quickly wrote down a number.

Mr. Green *really* wanted to win. He needed more than luck. He needed math.

He began calculating.
19 gumballs in a cup . . .
2 cups in a pint . . .
2 pints in a quart . . .
4 quarts in a gallon . . .
about 25 gallons
in the gumball jar . . .

So . . . 19 x 2 x 2 x 4 x 25 = 7,600.

Plus 317 (his favorite number)

for a grand total of 7,917.

Mr. Green wrote down his calculation.

The winners would be announced soon.

On the way home, Mr. Green imagined
gumballs everywhere—

gumball fountains,

gumball trees,

and a gumball car with gumball tires.

The world had never looked so wonderful.

At home, Mr. Green stretched out for a nap.

Mrs. Green began to paint—
she was inspired by all the gumball colors.
While she painted . . .

Mr. Green tossed and turned in his sleep.

He had a strange and crazy dream—

a spotty,
polka-dotty

gumball dream.

He was floating through a gumball galaxy . . .

without gravity (but with Mrs. Green by his side).

Suddenly, Mr. Green woke up—
someone was knocking at the door.

"CONGRATULATIONS!"

"You—yes, YOU,"
said the delivery man,
"are the Gumball-Guessing Champion!

I am pleased to present your prize—"

"Seven thousand nine hundred
and seventeen gumballs!"

"Yippee!
Hooray!
Yahooooo!"
said Mr. Green.
"And thank you!
It's a dream
come true."

Mrs. Green came running in—
she had heard all the excitement.
"I won first prize!" said Mr. Green.
"Congratulations," said Mrs. Green.
"How did you do it?"
"Math," said Mr. Green. "Lots of it.
And a little luck."

"Mrs. Green," said the delivery man,
"you are a gumball-guessing winner, too!
I am pleased to present you
the third-place prize—
and *heeeeeeerrrrrrrreee* it is!"

Inside was a little goldfish.
(He was one of Mrs. Green's
favorite colors—gold.)

"Congratulations!" said Mr. Green.

"What will you name him?"

"Gumball," said Mrs. Green.

"*Sir Gumball Goldfish the First.*

I can't wait to paint his portrait.

What will you do with *your* prize?"

"Oh, I have an idea," he said.

"Follow me."

"Look out below," said Mrs. Green.

"Here I come!"

"Goldfish and gumballs!" said Mr. Green.
"This really *is* our lucky day."

About the Author

Keith Baker has written and illustrated many well-loved picture books and early chapter books, including several about the charming and lovable Mr. and Mrs. Green. He lives in Seattle, Washington. Visit his website at www.KeithBakerBooks.com.

More Green Light Readers starring
Mr. and Mrs. Green!

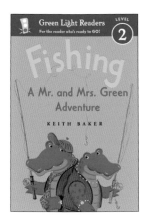

Fishing

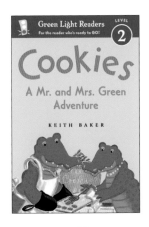

Cookies

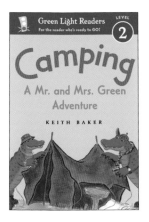

Camping

The Talent Show

Picture Books by Keith Baker

Big Fat Hen

Potato Joe

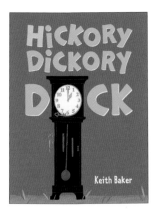

Hickory Dickory Dock

Hide and Snake

Who Is the Beast?

The Magic Fan

Quack and Count

Camping: A Mr. and Mrs. Green Adventure
Keith Baker

Cookies: A Mr. and Mrs. Green Adventure
Keith Baker

Fishing: A Mr. and Mrs. Green Adventure
Keith Baker

The Talent Show: A Mr. and Mrs.
Green Adventure
Keith Baker

George and Martha
James Marshall

George and Martha: Two Great Friends
James Marshall

George and Martha: Round and Round
James Marshall

George and Martha: Rise and Shine
James Marshall

George and Martha: One More Time
James Marshall

Martha Speaks: Haunted House
Susan Meddaugh

Martha Speaks: Play Ball
Susan Meddaugh

Martha Speaks: Toy Trouble
Susan Meddaugh

My Robot
Eve Bunting/Dagmar Fehlau

Soccer Song
Patricia Reilly Giff/Blanche Sims

Catch Me If You Can!/
¡A que no me alcanzas!
Bernard Most

A Butterfly Grows
Steven R. Swinburne

Daniel's Mystery Egg/
El misterioso huevo de Daniel
Alma Flor Ada/G. Brian Karas

Moving Day
Anthony G. Brandon/Wong Herbert Yee

Digger Pig and the Turnip/
Marranita Poco Rabo y el nabo
Caron Lee Cohen/Christopher Denise

The Chick That Wouldn't Hatch/
El pollito que no quería salir del huevo
Claire Daniel/Lisa Campbell Ernst

Get That Pest!/¡Agarren a ése!
Erin Douglas/Wong Herbert Yee

Snow Surprise
Lisa Campbell Ernst

On the Way to the Pond
Angela Shelf Madearis/Lorinda Bryan Cauley

Little Red Hen Gets Help
Kenneth Spengler/Margaret Spengler

Tumbleweed Stew/Sopa de matojos
Susan Stevens Crummel/Janet Stevens
Alma Flor Ada/F. Isabel Campoy